Maximus Mouse
and Friends

Brian Ogden

Illustrated by Elke Counsell

Scripture Union

First published 2000

Scripture Union, 207–209 Queensway, Bletchley, Milton
Keynes, MK2 2EB, England.

ISBN 1 85999 362 1

British Library Cataloguing-in-Publication Data.
A catalogue record of this book is available from the British
Library.

Printed and bound in Great Britain by
Creative Print and Design (Wales) Ebbw Vale.

Contents

Introduction

Maximus is a mouse who lives in
St Michael's Church. Maximus has many
friends who share his adventures and in this
book we meet six of them, together with
the forty-three mouselings. There's Patrick
and Paula, Barnabas the bat, Johann
Sebastian the organist's cat, Mr Toot the
owl and last of all Maximus' girlfriend
Caerphilly.

Each of Maximus' friends helps us to
understand about the fruits of the Holy
Spirit. You can find a list of these in the
Bible in Galatians chapter 5, verses 22 and
23. Just as a healthy tree produces good
fruit so the Holy Spirit helps us to have
joy, faithfulness, kindness, love, peace, self-
control and patience in our lives.

This is the tenth Maximus book and we
would like to thank all those who have

helped so much over the years – especially Elrose Hunter our editor and Elke Counsell our illustrator. We dedicate this book to them.

Finally we would like to thank all those who tell us they have enjoyed the stories and asked for more. We wish we could have invited you all to Maximus' wedding but the cake wasn't big enough!

Brian Ogden and Maximus Mouse

Chapter One

A good day

It was the school holidays and the mouselings were having a great time. They were everywhere. Some of the mouselings, led by Percy, were in the graveyard of St Michael's Church playing pawball.

Shoot!

But Percy's brother Peregrine missed the ball completely and fell over on his back. The other mouselings just stood around laughing.

At the back of the church another group had piled up some of the hymn books. Petronella had found some string.

Tie it on like this and let yourself go!

Another group had climbed into the pulpit. From the top it was a long way down. Petunia had borrowed Paula's umbrella.

"Hold on tight and jump. The brolly's like a parachute," she told Philip.

It was then that Maximus came out of the vestry and saw what was happening.

Philip was balancing on the edge of the pulpit. The brolly was waving about like a flag on a windy day. Philip wobbled forward. Maximus was sure he would fall. Then he moved backwards and with a tiny scream disappeared inside the pulpit.

Maximus rushed over. He arrived just in time to see Philip standing up and rubbing his head.

"Come on, Uncle Maximus," said Petunia. "You have a go."

"No way," said Maximus. "And I don't think you should be doing it anyway. Do your parents know you're doing this?"

"Well, not exactly," said Petunia. "But they do know we are having lots of fun."

At that moment Philip floated down with the umbrella and crashed into Maximus.

Maximus picked Philip up, shook himself, and left the mouselings to their brollychuting. A little further down the church another group of mouselings had borrowed a large sheet of paper from the

Sunday School cupboard. The paper lay over one of the stones in the aisle. Using wax crayons they were rubbing over the paper.

"That's really clever," said Maximus.

Slowly a picture of an old knight was showing up on the paper. Under his feet were some words.

Here lieth the body of Sir Ernest Hedderwick, Knight.

"We call him Dead Ernest," said Philomena, who seemed to be leading the group. "We like rubbing him. Do you want to try, Uncle Maximus?"

A little later that morning, Maximus caught up with Patrick and Paula.

"Your mouselings seem to be enjoying themselves," he said.

"Do you know, Maximus," said Paula, "they can teach us a lot about being happy. They have a joy that we grown-up mice seem to lose. You can see this joy in their faces. You can hear it in the way they squeak."

At that moment all the mouselings marched through the church singing their favourite song.

"Once a jolly mouseling joined in a silly
    song,

With his brothers and sisters, forty-three...
And they sang as they watched and waited
    for their tea to come...
Plenty of cheddar for you and me!
Plenty of cheddar, plenty of cheddar,
Plenty of cheddar for you and me.
And they sang as they watched and waited
    for their tea to come...
Plenty of cheddar for you and me!"

Loving Father,

You give us so many wonderful things. Give us joyful hearts in return. Amen.

Chapter Two

Rollerblades, a duvet and a mouse

"I can still do it," said Maximus to himself. "I'm sure I can."

Maximus was having a tidy-up in the vestry. He had collected so many bits and pieces over the years. Now he didn't know what to do with them. There were magazines he hadn't thrown away like *Mouse Beautiful* and *Rodents' Own*. There were at least nine *Tom and Jerry* annuals. There was a rather smelly pair of old pawball boots. Right at the bottom of the pile Maximus found the skateboard.

It was the board he and Patrick had used all that time ago.

He remembered how he had skated right down the aisle of the church and crashed into the font.

Patrick had had to pick him up and patch him up. But this time it would be different. This time he was older. This time he knew what he was doing.

Maximus took the board out into the church. He put one paw on the board and one on the floor. He gave a big push and...

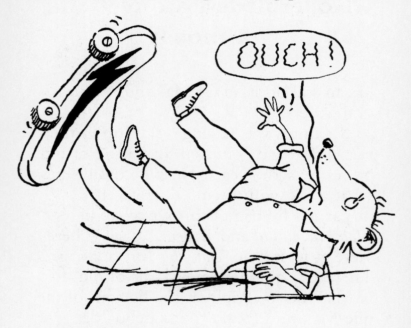

Patrick came rushing out of the Sunday School cupboard.

"Whatever's the matter?" he said, as he nearly fell over Maximus.

"Just a little accident," said Maximus. "I was just checking to see if the board still worked."

"Perhaps we should check if *you* still work!" said Patrick.

Patrick gently helped Maximus to his paws and took him back to the vestry.

"Patrick, you're always there to help," said Maximus. "Thank you."

Please take care, Maximus

The next day a mysterious parcel arrived in the post for Maximus. He took it from the postmouse and hid it behind his back in case anymouse saw it. In the vestry he tore off the wrapping. There lying in front of him was a box. On the outside of the box Maximus saw the words...

The rollerblades looked twice as good as the advert. He lifted them out of the box and sat down. Carefully he put one on each front paw. He slid one paw forward and back. Very smooth. He did the same with the other one. Fantastic.

Very slowly and very quietly Maximus skated down through the church and out into the graveyard. By the time he reached the gate into the road he was travelling fast. Too fast. Maximus, as usual, had not stopped to find out how to stop.

He tried to grab one of the gate-posts as he passed.

All that did was to turn him sideways so, instead of skating on the road, he was now skating down the pavement.

It really was down the pavement
because the church was at the top of a hill.

A lady was very surprised to see a
mouse pass her on rollerblades.

"Grr…" growled a large Alsatian dog as
Maximus skated right underneath him.

At the bottom of the hill was Patrick. He had just been shopping in Barks and Dentures. He had bought a beautiful new pink duvet as a birthday present for Paula. Patrick heard Maximus yell. He looked up in time to see a familiar mouse racing towards him.

Patrick thought very quickly. He tore open the bag. He grabbed the beautiful new pink duvet and shook it out.

Very soon there was a large heap on the ground. It was made up of a pink duvet, a pair of Geronimouse In-Line Rollerblades and a mouse.

The mouse spoke.

"Patrick, you've done it again. You're always there when I need you."

> You're the most faithful friend anymouse could want!

Patrick took Maximus back to the church. Patrick then had some very difficult explaining to do to Paula.

Loving Lord God,
Thank you, that even when we forget you, you are always a faithful friend to us. Amen.

Chapter Three

Trombone with a flea biting it

"Oh, ouch," groaned Maximus.

As Maximus woke, the church clock struck three times.

He had been woken up by a sharp pain. It was in his left leg. He moved his leg around but it didn't help. The pain was

getting worse. Maximus was very worried.
No one would hear him if he called out.
Patrick and Paula were the nearest but the
Sunday School cupboard was on the other
side of the church.

The church clock struck four times.
There were still hours before anymouse
would be about. He couldn't just lie there
all that time. Then he had an idea.

Under his bed he kept a torch. He used
it for reading in bed. He had been reading
the night before.

It was one of the Mousebumps books
about a mouse called Wych-hazel.

Maximus kept turning the torch on and off, hoping someone would see the signal.

For a long time nothing happened. The battery got weaker and Maximus gave up hope of anyone coming. Just as the torch faded Maximus heard a strange noise coming from the window. It was too dark to see what had made the noise. There was silence. Then there was a bump as the something landed on the floor. Maximus was terrified. What could the something be? Was he going to end up as an early breakfast for something that went bump in the night? Then he heard a voice.

Maximus, are you all right? I saw the light at the window as I was passing.

"Excuse me, please," stuttered Maximus, "but who are you?"

"It's Johann Sebastian," said the cat. "I didn't mean to frighten you but I thought you might be in trouble."

Johann Sebastian is the organist's cat at St Michael's Church.

"Oh, Johann, I am so pleased to see you," said Maximus. "I woke up with this awful pain in my leg. I couldn't move. I was hoping someone would see my signals."

Johann found the light in the vestry and put it on. Maximus looked very unhappy.

"Right," said Johann, "I shall take you to the Casualty department at the hospital."

Johann stopped from time to time to see

Hold tight, Maximus. We've got a long way to go.

if Maximus was all right. After what
seemed like for ever to Maximus they
arrived at the hospital. Johann left
Maximus and found a nurse.

"My friend has a very bad pain in his
leg," said Johann.

She looked at his leg then went to call a

doctor.

"Well now," said the doctor, "you have
thrombophlebitis. It can be very painful. I
will give you some tablets. Take two now
and then two twice a day. They will help
to take the pain away."

Very carefully Johann Sebastian carried

Maximus back to the church. By the time they got there Maximus was beginning to feel better. Johann put Maximus to bed. He got him a really fresh hymn sheet for breakfast then, leaving Maximus asleep, tip-pawed quietly out of the vestry.

Maximus woke up much later in the day to find Patrick and Paula standing by his bed.

"Better, thank you," said Maximus.

We hear you've been pawly in the night.

How are you now, Maximus?

LONG LIFE BATTERIES

"Johann Sebastian was wonderful. He was so kind. He carried me all the way to the hospital, brought me back and put me to bed. No mouse could have been kinder than Johann."

"He is a very kind cat," said Paula.

"He sometimes takes the mouselings to school if they're late."

"Oh, by the way," said Maximus, "I've got a 'trombone with a flea biting it' in my leg."

Dear God,
Thank you for all those who are kind to us in so many ways. Help us to show kindness to others. Amen.

Chapter Four

Mouseing Sunday

On their way home from school, three mouselings crept into Maximus' vestry.

"Uncle Max," said Percy, "we need your help. Next Sunday is Mouseing Sunday. It's the day when we do something special for mouse mums."

I remember I used to take my mum tea in bed on Mouseing Sunday!

"Well," said Posie, "that's the problem
– there are forty-three of us mouselings
and Mum doesn't really want forty-three
cups of tea in bed."

"So," said Pomegranate, "me, Posie and
Percy thought we would ask you what we
should do."

"We could take her to a pawball
match," said Percy hopefully.
"Mousehampton United are playing on
Saturday – I bet she'd love that."

"NO!" said Posie loudly. "Mum would
not like that. We want to do something
SHE would like. She's always doing things
for us."

"Well," said Maximus, stroking his
whiskers, "sorry Percy, but I think Posie's
right. I don't think Paula would really
want to go to a pawball match. I think she
would like a special surprise meal... and
some promises."

"I like cooking," said Pomegranate.
"We could make her a Mousing Sunday
cake. But... but she'll see it if we cook it at
home."

"Come here then," said Maximus.
"You could get the meal ready here
without Paula knowing."

"I'm not sure I like the sound of promises," said Percy. "What do you mean, Uncle Maximus?"

Maximus and the three mouselings sat and talked about Mouseing Sunday for a long time.

During the next few days small parties of mouselings went into Maximus' vestry after school.

Paula never guessed that anything was going on.

On Mouseing Sunday, after the Family Service, Maximus went over to Paula.

"Paula, please follow me," said
Maximus. Paula looked a little surprised
but she followed Maximus to the vestry.

Behind them on the table was the most
delicious meal - organic music sandwiches,
candlewax quiche, Church Notice salad,
ant-flavoured crisps and dew cola to drink.
Paula was squeakless.

"It's a wonderful surprise," she said,
when at last she found her squeak.

At the end of the meal Paula, Patrick
and Maximus sat down. Percy came and
stood in front of them.

"On Mouseing Sunday we want to say

a big 'thank you', Mum, for everything you do for us. But we also want to make some promises which we will try to keep."

At that moment Peregrine walked forward. He was holding a piece of paper.

He was followed by Posie holding a paper with these words...

Next came Peter. His paper read...

Then Prudence arrived with this promise...

Last of all came Petronella with all the other mouselings. Her paper was in the shape of a heart. All the mouselings joined together in reading the words aloud

By this time Paula didn't know whether to laugh or cry.

"Well," she said, "I love you all too — very much. Thank you for a wonderful surprise. I wonder if Uncle Maximus knew anything about it?"

"Er, ... shall we leave the mouselings to clear up?" suggested Maximus, as he led Paula and Patrick out of the vestry.

Loving God,
Thank you for all those who look after
   us —
for all that they do for us,
for all that they mean to us,
for all their love for us.
Help us to show our love in return -
by what we do,
by what we say,
and by who we are. Amen

Chapter Five

Bring your umbrella with you

"Why do you sleep all day?" asked Maximus. "I mean, most animals are awake during the day and sleep when it's dark."

It was late in the evening and Maximus had gone out to watch the sun set. As the world got darker an old friend swooped down and landed on one of the grave stones.

"It's like this, Maximus," said Mr Toot, "I like peace. During the day everything is so busy and so noisy. Humans with their mobile phones, cows mooing, sheep bleating and even mice squeaking!"

"Yes, it can be a bit noisy during the day," agreed Maximus. "Mouselings playing games, buses going past the church, the television talking at you. I suppose if you want peace then the night is a good time for it."

"Why don't you try it, Maximus?" asked Mr Toot. "I tell you what – I'll meet you tomorrow evening. We can spend the night together and I'll show you how peaceful it really is. By the way, please bring an umbrella with you."

Maximus went to bed. The next morning he was woken by the vicar banging his case down on the vestry table. Then the organist came in to practise for the Sunday services.

Things got worse when the ladies who cleaned the church came in with their noisy vacuum cleaner.

After that the mouselings came home
and started a game just outside Maximus'
window. It was anything but peaceful.

Earlier Maximus had wondered if he had
done the right thing in agreeing to go out
all night with Mr Toot. Now he was quite
sure – there was no peace during the day.

As the sun set, Maximus left the vestry
and went out. He remembered to take his
umbrella but as it was a dry night he didn't
think he would need it. Soon Mr Toot
joined him in the darkening graveyard.

Do you like flying?

I've flown before
but never by owl.
You will take care
won't you?

"Of course I will," said Mr Toot, "but just in case you should let go, remember your umbrella. If you find yourself falling, just open the umbrella and you'll land safely."

Maximus wasn't too sure about this and decided it would be much better to hang on to Mr Toot.

Maximus shut his eyes. When he opened them a few moments later he was flying high above the church tower. Mr Toot could see much better than Maximus in the dark.

"This is just amazing," said Maximus. "It's so peaceful."

Mr Toot landed gently on a branch of the old oak tree which grew in the corner of the churchyard. Maximus climbed off and sat beside the old owl.

It was amazing. The moon was slowly climbing up her ladder to the top of the sky. The whole world looked calm and beautiful.

"Yes," said Mr Toot, "you see, a lot of animals chase around all the time. They make a lot of noise. They never stop. They don't find a peaceful place like this and enjoy it. Humans need peace but they're not very good at finding it."

Maximus and Mr Toot sat for a long time on the branch.

At last, as the sun started to get out of bed, Mr Toot took Maximus home.

"Thank you, Mr Toot," said Maximus. "Now I understand why you sleep in the day and stay awake at night. You've taught me how important peace is."

Then he went to bed and had a very peaceful day's sleep.

Jesus, Prince of peace,
Help us not to rush about all the time but to stop and take time to find you in peace and quiet. Amen.

Chapter Six

Barnabas goes batty

Barnabas never could get Maximus' name right. Barnabas, the church bat, and Maximus, the church mouse, both live and work in St Michael's Church but they don't see each other very often. The reason for this is that Maximus looks after the church during the day and Barnabas during the night.

"Thank you, Barnabas, for dropping in," said Maximus. "Yes, you see, I'm going away for a few days. Going to visit some cousins in Mousehole in Cornwall. Haven't seen them for ages."

"Delightful part of the country," said Barnabas. "Hope you have a splendid time."

"Well, with me being away," said Maximus, "there won't be anyone to look after the church during the day. I was hoping you would keep an eye on things – that is, if you are awake of course."

"Humph," said Barnabas. "That means there'll be silly humans about. Never can get on with humans. They get in my hair – or is it the other way round? I get in theirs!"

Maximus went off to pack. He remembered his swimming trunks, clean socks, toothbrush and paste and a book to read on the train.

Patrick and Paula and all the mouselings wished him a happy holiday.

"I do hope that Barnabas manages all right," said Maximus, as he waved goodbye.

From high up in the church tower Barnabas saw Maximus leave. A few minutes later he saw a large group of ladies walking up the church path and into the building.

"Now what do they want?" said Barnabas to himself. "Minibus didn't tell me about this."

Barnabas launched himself from the hole in the belfry into the church. The ladies were sitting quietly in the pews. Then one of them looked up. She nudged her neighbour.

The scream made all the other ladies look up and point to Barnabas. This made the little bat very angry. He knew it was very bad manners to point at bats or at people. He would teach them a lesson.

Barnabas forgot what Maximus had told him. He swooped up and down over the ladies. There was panic. Some of them rushed to the door trying to get out. Some of them tried to get under the pews. Some of them stood there shouting and pointing.

The vicar, who had come in to start the service, tried to calm things down.

Ladies, please! It's only Barnabas our church bat.

There was so much noise going on that no one could hear him. It was only when Barnabas realised that he had lost his self-control and flew back into the belfry that things started to quieten down. The little bat felt very ashamed.

After a few more minutes Barnabas heard the organist playing and the service started. It was an afternoon the ladies would talk about for years to come.

Maximus came back from his holidays looking very well. He brought some Mousehole rock for Patrick, Paula, the mouselings and Barnabas.

And Barnabas went on to tell Maximus
what happened.

Loving Father,
It is very hard to keep our self-control when we
are cross or tempted to do something wrong.
Please give us your strength to help us. Amen.

Chapter Seven

Happily ever after

"Well," Maximus said, "we were very good friends at mouseling school."

"But then Caerphilly moved to Wales with her parents. She got married and had

lots of mouselings of her own. One day
she wrote to tell me that her husband
Owen had died."

"That's sad," said Posie. "But Uncle
Maximus, why haven't you ever got
married?"

Maximus looked embarrassed.

"I suppose it's because I've always loved
Caerphilly. We were such good friends and
I missed her dreadfully when she went
away."

"But now she's coming back," said
Percy.

Perhaps Uncle Maximus will get
married after all! I've always
wanted to be a bridesmouse.

"If Uncle Maximus got married there would have to be twenty-one bridesmice," said Percy. "All your sisters would want to be there."

"And twenty-two pagemice," added Posie.

Maximus crept away while the mouselings went on talking about him and Caerphilly. It had been such a long time since he had seen her. But her letter was quite clear. She would be coming up from Wales on holiday and would like to stay with him. He must get the guest shoe-box ready.

"That means cleaning and dusting and tidying and clearing out and getting food in and washing the curtains and..."

During the next few days Maximus was a very busy mouse. Some of the mouselings helped him. Well, that's what they were supposed to do. Posie spilt water everywhere and Percy broke a favourite vase.

After an hour or so Maximus thought it would be quicker to get on by himself. At the end of a really busy day Maximus went to bed. But not to sleep. He lay under his little duvet thinking.

"I've been waiting and hoping
Caerphilly would come back for ages," he
thought. "I love Patrick, Paula and the
mouselings but I've always hoped I would
see Caerphilly again. She's a very special
friend."

The sun shining through the vestry
window woke Maximus as the church
clock struck ten times.

Oh, no! I'm going to be late! Caerphilly's train is due in half an hour.

Maximus struggled into his best clothes. He put his shoes on the wrong paws and had to change them. He rushed out of the church and scampered as fast as he could to the station.

The train drew in as Maximus reached the platform. One of the doors opened and there was Caerphilly. Maximus couldn't believe his eyes. Caerphilly had hardly changed at all. She was still the Caerphilly he had waited for so patiently.

It's so good to see you after all this time!

Maximus nodded his head. He was too happy to squeak. All that waiting had been worthwhile. Caerphilly was here and Maximus didn't want her ever to go away again.

Back at St Michael's Church he introduced Caerphilly to Patrick, Paula and the mouselings. Paula had made a special dinner. It was Sermon Notes-in-the-Hole with candle wax chips followed by Confetti Multi-coloured Ice-cream.

"Thank you so much," said Caerphilly. "That was delicious."

"Perhaps there'll be some more confetti soon?"

"Percy behave yourself!" said Patrick. "I'm sorry about my rude son."

Maximus and Caerphilly left Patrick and Paula doing the washing-up... with the help of Percy. They wandered out of the church into the graveyard.

"...er, Caerphilly, I'm not good at saying this," stuttered Maximus, "'cos I've never done it before, but I have been waiting ever so long to do it, but could you, I mean, would you...

Caerphilly looked at Maximus. It seemed like for ever before she answered.

"Yes, please," she squeaked.

There was a wonderful wedding.

There were twenty-one bridemice and twenty-two pagemice. Patrick was Maximus' best mouse.

Paula prepared a delicious wedding breakfast.

60

"Caerphilly has made me the happiest mouse in the whole world," said Maximus. "It only goes to show what can happen if you are patient."

And Maximus and Caerphilly lived happily ever after.

Loving Father,

We always want everything to happen at once. Teach us to be patient — patient with you, patient with other people and patient with ourselves. Amen.

Some more books to enjoy!

Tales of Young Maximus Mouse
Brian Ogden

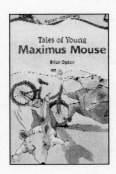

"Do you remember that day at school when we swapped the cheese for plasticine?" asked Maximus. "Too right," said Mick. "All the mouselings and teachers picked up the plasticine and took a big bite. It was a pity they caught us though! We missed our playtimes for a whole week." Maximus Mouse lets us into the secrets of his life as a mouseling.

ISBN 1 85999 328 1
Price £3.50

Available from your local Christian bookshop

Shorty
Christine Wright

Lindy and her family visit an African animal theme park, with exciting roller coaster rides and a Safari Island. Join in the fun!

ISBN 1 85999 255 3
Price £3.50

Bernard Bunting's Missing Birthday
Ro Willoughby

Bernard's birthday seems to have been forgotten in the excitement of preparing for Christmas – or so Bernard thinks. Does God know about this and does he care? Bernard is in for a big surprise.

ISBN 1 85999 327 3
Price £3.50

Available from your local Christian bookshop